First published in the United States 1990 by

Atomium Books Inc.
Suite 300
1013 Centre Road
Wilmington, DE 19805.

First edition published in German by K. Thienemanns Verlag, Stuttgart-Wien, 1988,
under the title "Der Rote Sessel."

Printed and bound in Belgium by
Color Print Graphix, Antwerp.
First U.S. Edition
ISBN 1-56182-034-2
2 4 6 8 10 9 7 5 3 1

The Red Armchair

by Achim Bröger and Manfred Schlüter

English adaptation by Philomena Korbutt

atomium books

Patti's next door neighbors were having a big garage sale and Patti went to look at all the things they had for sale. She found a washing machine, a tall lamp, some old toys . . . and a big red armchair.

"That could be a cozy place for me!" she thought.

She rushed back home and dragged her family over to show them what she'd found.

Dad looked serious. "You know, it'll take some work to fix it up."

"But it's only $10!" encouraged Patti.

Mom thought hard. "It's too good a bargain to pass up," she said. "Let's buy it!"

They paid the neighbor. Then Mom, Dad, Patti, and her two brothers carried the armchair into their house.

They dusted, scrubbed, beat, and vacuumed the armchair until it was clean and bright red again — as good as new!

"All that hard work has made me tired," said Dad. "This armchair is just what I need to help me relax." He settled down into the soft cushion. Soon his eyes were closed as he dozed off.

"That does look comfortable," agreed Mom. She snuggled onto Dad's lap.

Little Tim scrambled quickly onto her knee.

"Wait for me!" said Bobby, as he jumped onto the back of the chair.

"This isn't fair," thought Patti. "Everyone is using this chair but me."

She climbed onto the arm and began to rock the heavy chair back and forth.

It began to creeeaaak.

"Whoa!" said Dad. "This load is too much for our new chair. EVERYBODY OFF!"

Patti smiled.

When the coast was clear, Patti crept back to the red armchair with a helmet, a sword, and a flag.

"This is MY castle," said Patti. "And I will protect it from all attackers."

From the tower, she could see two invaders coming up the hill and crossing the moat. The castle shook as they climbed its walls.

The soldiers yelled and waved their swords so much that Patti had to escape through a secret tunnel.

When she looked back, the invaders were taking down her flag.

"I'll be back," she promised.

Patti waited until the armchair was empty again. This time she decided to camouflage it with plants. Now it was a jungle!

Everything was peaceful and sweet-smelling as Patti sat under the leaves.

But there, behind her red armchair, snuck two hunters carrying poison spears.

"Armchair. Armchair. Armchair. . . ." they chanted.

How would she escape?

She reached high for a vine and swung herself wildly through the leaves.

Patti was safe . . . but the hunters had captured her red armchair.

A little later Mom came in and saw that the chair was empty.

"Oh good," she said. "I've got time to read the newspaper and relax."

She plopped down into the red softness.

Patti looked at Bobby and Tim. They knew they couldn't let this dragon take over their red mountain.

The three knights put on their shining armor and surrounded the beast, charging at her from different directions.

The dragon roared. Huge, hot flames billowed out of her nostrils.

But the fearless knights closed in on her, closer and closer, until — tired and worn out — the dragon retreated from the red mountain.

"Everybody wants my armchair. If only I could drive it off to a secret spot," thought Patti.

Quickly she got some tires, a steering wheel, and a stick shift.

She leapt into her turbo-charged racing car and took off as fast as lightning.

Patti drove way out into the country. In the mirror she could see a blue car with two people chasing her. It would be easy to outrun them.

She was speeding around a very sharp corner when she suddenly lost control. One of her back wheels had come off!

Patti ended up in a ditch on the side of the road.

When she looked up, she saw her brothers examining the overturned car.

Just then the doorbell rang and in walked Mr. Jones, their neighbor. He had come to tell them about how well his garage sale had gone.

He didn't seem to recognize the big red armchair when he sat down in it.

As Mr. Jones talked to Patti's parents, his smelly cigarette ashes fell onto the arm of her chair. Patti was shocked!

"No wonder this chair was in such bad shape," she thought. "I wish he'd leave."

After two cups of tea and too many cigarettes, Mr. Jones finally left.

The armchair was safe.

As Patti carefully dusted off the chair again, she spotted her brothers sneaking around the corner.

Quickly she set the chair up as a big red wild-West stagecoach. Then she lassoed the rocking horse and was on her way.

Two braves followed right behind her. With their strong bows they shot a constant stream of arrows at her. One whizzed right by Patti's left ear.

She realized she'd better give up quietly.

Patti pulled on the reins and grumbled to herself as the horse slowed to a stop.

Soon her brothers became tired of playing on the stagecoach and left the room. Patti had a new idea and worked fast. She gathered together all sorts of things.

Soon her red airplane was ready. She jumped into the cockpit and took off.

Patti flew around, enjoying the wide open blue sky. At last she was all alone.

Just as she was thinking how wonderful it felt, two huge black birds dove in front of her. They swooped and pecked at her until she was forced to jump from the plane.

"It was a good thing I remembered to bring a parachute!" Patti thought, as she floated back down to her living room.

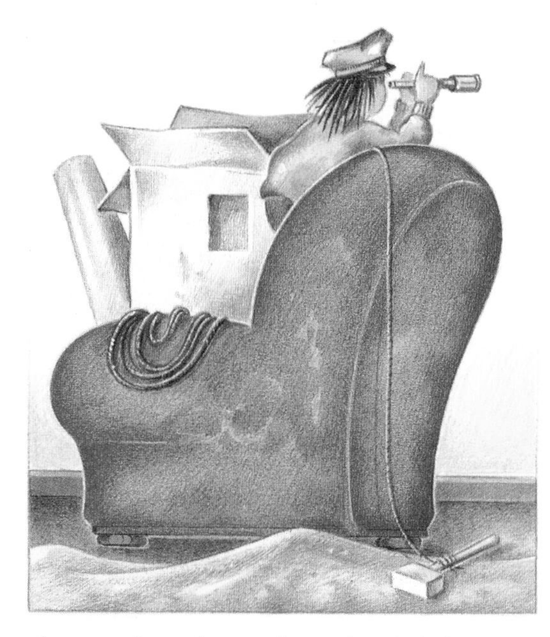

This time Patti returned to the armchair with some boxes and rope. She turned it into a small, but very strong, tugboat. If she couldn't lose them in the air, she'd head out to sea.

She chugged along happily, widening the gap between the shore and her boat.

But what was that spot on the horizon?

Patti picked up her spyglass and scanned the waves. It was two pirates! And they were closing in on her.

"Surrender, or we'll sink your boat!" they shouted.

The red tugboat had no guns. What could she do?

Patti took a deep breath, jumped overboard, and swam safely ashore.

The room was quiet again when Patti pulled the armchair in front of the door and turned it into a beautiful throne.

There she sat, in her shiny crown, ready for anyone who dared to challenge her. Patti was the Queen!

She thought about her magnificent palace and the grand ball she was giving that night.

As she daydreamed of how beautiful she would look in her silk gown, two servants snuck from behind the big red throne.

One sprang upon her suddenly!

Patti was so startled, she fell right off the throne and lost her crown.

When Patti came back into the room, no one else was there. She pulled herself onto the chair, exhausted. She needed time to think.

A little while later, her brothers found her snuggled up with her eyes closed.

"I think she's asleep," whispered Tim. "Maybe we'd better leave her alone."

As they tiptoed away from the chair, Patti opened one eye — just a little — and smiled.

Then she dozed off. It had been a busy day.

Finally Patti had found a way to enjoy the red armchair all by herself . . . at least for a while.